THURSDAY

By **Ann Bonwill**

Illustrated by **Kayla Harren**

two lions

Published by Two Lions, New York

www.apub.com

Amazon, the Amazon logo, and Two Lions are trademarks of Amazon.com, Inc., or its affiliates.

ISBN-13: 9781542032896 (hardcover)
ISBN-10: 154203289X (hardcover)

The illustrations are rendered in digital media.

Book design by Abby Dening
Printed in China
First Edition

1 3 5 7 9 10 8 6 4 2

For Ness, a true friend every day of the week
—A. B.

For Marietta—thank you for making this book happen
—K. H.

They told her on a Thursday.

Thursday used to be her most favorite day because of art class with Mr. Chen

and Popsicles in the cafeteria.

THURSDAY LUNCH
chicken fingers
broccoli, corn potato
popsicle

Now it was her most unfavorite day.
Because after that Thursday, everything was going to be different.

She tried to be brave,
but inside she was melting.

I knew what it was like to melt . . .

and to be saved by a friend.

So I came to stay
for a while.

I took her to all her favorite places.

She laughed at the prairie dogs
guarding their tunnel city.

She ate cotton candy till
her tongue turned blue.

She hung upside down with
her hair touching the ground.

She pet the soft, velvety wing of the stingray as it glided by.
And, for a minute, her heart felt like a sunrise.

It was a perfect day.

Until it wasn't.

I didn't know what else to do,
so I simply stayed with her.

chirp!

chirp!

chirp!

Sometimes that's enough.

Then ... eventually ... she found a way to help another.

Sometimes that's the best.

We watched for a while until ...

she started gathering things too: old scraps,
tiny treasures, memories from her life before.

She found a box to build her nest in,
and she decorated it with stars.

It was small enough to travel back and forth
but big enough to hold her heart.

The truck came on
a Thursday.

It took some of her things one way...

and some of them another.

After that,
everything *was* different.

Sometimes better.

And sometimes worse.

Until Thursday became
just Thursday again.

That's when I knew it was time for me to go.

But I am always with her
when she needs me.

Especially on Thursday.